George Sumner

An Oration Delivered before the Municipal Authorities of the City of Boston, July 4, 1859

SALZWASSER
VERLAG

George Sumner

An Oration Delivered before the Municipal Authorities of the City of Boston, July 4, 1859

Reprint of the original, first published in 1859.

1st Edition 2022 | ISBN: 978-3-37513-228-6

Verlag (Publisher): Salzwasser Verlag GmbH, Zeilweg 44, 60439 Frankfurt, Deutschland
Vertretungsberechtigt (Authorized to represent): E. Roepke, Zeilweg 44, 60439 Frankfurt, Deutschland
Druck (Print): Books on Demand GmbH, In de Tarpen 42, 22848 Norderstedt, Deutschland

ORATION.

AN

ORATION

DELIVERED BEFORE THE

MUNICIPAL AUTHORITIES

OF THE CITY OF BOSTON,

JULY 4, 1859,

BY GEORGE SUMNER.

SECOND EDITION.

BOSTON:

TICKNOR AND FIELDS.

M DCCC LIX.

CITY OF BOSTON.

In Common Council, July 21, 1859.

ORDERED : That the thanks of the City Council be, and they hereby are presented to GEORGE SUMNER, Esq., for the eloquent Oration by him delivered before the Municipal Authorities on the occasion of the Celebration of the Eighty-Third Anniversary of the Declaration of American Independence, and that a copy of said Oration be requested for publication.

Sent up for concurrence.

J. P. BRADLEE, *President.*

In Board of Aldermen, July 25, 1859.

Passed in concurrence.

SILAS PEIRCE, *Chairman.*

Approved, July 27, 1859.

F. W. LINCOLN, JR., *Mayor.*

PREFACE.

HONORED by the request of the City Council to speak, in the name of Boston, on the Fourth of July, it seemed to me proper on that occasion to discuss some of our obligations, as Americans, to other nations and to ourselves.

The facts then stated, which bear upon the aid given our country in its Revolutionary struggle, were verified by the examination of original documents in the archives of the State Department at Washington, of the French Ministry of Foreign Affairs at Paris, and of the Spanish government at Seville and Madrid; and also of papers in the hands of the executor of Caron de Beaumarchais, the agent of the first benefactions of France.*

In giving to Spain the credit of having projected the Armed Neutrality of 1780, I am aware that I may seem to have differed from many writers on International Law. The statement, however, was not lightly made, nor without documentary evidence to sustain it.

---

* As the recent biographer of Beaumarchais, M. de Loménie, has charged the United States with ingratitude to him, I take this opportunity publicly to state, that having drawn the attention of his executor to the first accusations of M. de Loménie, in the *Revue des Deux Mondes*, that gentleman declared to me, that every just claim of Beaumarchias had been " fully, largely, and generously paid by the United States ; " and this declaration he offered to repeat, in his official capacity, before a Notary Public.

Of what was said concerning the position of European countries, I have nothing to alter on account of the truce of Villafranca.

As regards recent events in our own country, speaking in the name of a law-abiding people, I felt it my duty to raise a warning voice against conduct which the wisest jurists in the land have denounced, as tending to bring the tribunals of the law into disrespect. Speaking in the name of those whose ancestors made sacrifices to secure liberty founded on law— and who believe an essential guaranty of that liberty to consist in the separation of the legislative, executive and judicial functions—I should have been recreant to my trust did I fail to speak of acts which tended, if not to confound those functions, at least to destroy their harmonious balance. Venerating the Constitution, I could not stand dumb in presence of the earnest appeal of the Senior Judge of the Supreme Court— the companion upon the bench of Marshall — Mr. Justice McLean, who, alarmed at the usurpations of the Chief Justice, and other of his junior colleagues, exclaimed in the Dred Scott case: "Have the impressive lessons of practical wisdom become lost to the present generation? If the great and fundamental principles of our Government are never to be settled, there can be no lasting prosperity. The Constitution will become a floating waif on the billows of popular excitement." Yielding to no one in respect for our judicial system—and keenly alive to the importance of that respect being universal—I felt it my duty to invoke the supreme tribunal of the land—the Sovereign Public Opinion of the country—to aid in awakening a portion of the Judiciary to a sense of self-respect — the basis of respect from others.

Jefferson in a letter to Edward Livingston, of 25th March, 1825, says: "Your code for Louisiana will range your name with the sages of antiquity. One single object will entitle you to the endless gratitude of society; that of *restraining judges from usurping legislation.* . . . Experience has proved that impeachment in our forms is completely inefficient. A regard for reputation and the judgment of the world, may sometimes be felt where conscience is dormant, or indolence inexcitable."

Story also recognized as the High Court of Appeals of our country, "its intelligence, its integrity, its learning and its manliness."

In addressing myself to these, I followed my convictions of duty; being true to which I felt that I was true to Boston. — I was happy moreover in the certainty that even so humble a voice as my own, when speaking for the purity and dignity of the Judiciary, had the cordial support of the members of every "healthy political organization" in the Republic. G. S.

Boston, 1st August, 1859.

2

ORATION.

EIGHTY-THREE years have passed since the delegates of thirteen feeble colonies proclaimed the immortal truths of that Declaration to which we have just listened. This act, pregnant with consequences to all mankind, stands in history as the record of the birth of a new nation.

In 1776 the great powers of Europe were at peace, and England was at full liberty to throw on our shores the whole force of her arms.

In the great contest which ensued — a contest for self-government and for the equal rights of man — perils were encountered and sufferings endured, which we, calmly enjoying their fruits, remember with gratitude to the men who toiled for us, and with fealty to the principles which they proclaimed.

The struggle was long and unequal; and when the enemy succeeded in gaining possession of New York, the timid began to falter. All eyes were now turned to Europe. Delegates had been already despatched to seek the assistance of France, and their hopes were not disappointed. One million of francs were given from the French treasury; cannon and military stores furnished from the arsenals of France; other stores to the value of a million of dollars placed in colonial ports accessible to our vessels; and a series of friendly acts commenced which, on the 6th of February, 1778, were consummated in a treaty of alliance, and in a declaration by which France bound herself to make no peace with England until the independence of the United States was fully recognized.

But it was not France alone which came to our aid. During that summer of '76, one of those brave men who were the creators of the naval glory of our country, Captain John Lee, of Marblehead, cruising under a commission from Congress, having taken and sent home five valuable prizes, and finding it necessary to refit and obtain supplies and munitions of war, entered the port of Bilbao in Spain. The captains of two of his prizes and a part of their crews were on board. These officers immediately protested against their capture, and had Capt. Lee arrested on a charge of piracy. The local authorities sent the documents of the case to Madrid, together with the commission granted by this new and unknown power. Here was a critical juncture in our affairs. On the decision of the Spanish Ministry depended, not alone the fate of Capt. Lee, but whether some of the most important ports in Europe

should be opened or closed to our cruisers and pri-
vateers. The English Minister in Spain brought all
his influence to bear against us. At this moment
the Declaration of the Fourth of July reached Madrid.
The complaint against Capt. Lee was dismissed ; supplies for his ship, and aid in repairing it were furnished ; and public declaration made that in Spanish
ports the new flag of America was as free and as
welcome as was the old and haughty flag of England.*

This open act of friendship had been preceded by
another. On the 27th June, 1776, the Spanish Minister of Foreign Affairs sent to Count Aranda, Am-
bassador of Spain, in Paris, one million francs, as a
free gift for the American Colonies; † and on the
11th August this million was paid over to the agent,
with whom Silas Deane and Arthur Lee, as delegates
of Congress, were in treaty for the shipment of arms
and supplies.

But this was not all. Cargoes of military stores
were sent to us from Bilbao; then the hint was

---

* Cooper, in his *Naval History of the United States*, seems entirely to
have overlooked this interesting episode. Captain Lee was a brother of
Colonel William Lee, for many years Collector of Salem, the same to
whom Washington proposed the place of Adjutant General of the Revolutionary Army, before offering it to Colonel Timothy Pickering. Silas
Deane, in his despatch of 17th October, 1776, to the Committee of Secret
Correspondence of Congress, erroneously describes Captain Lee as of New-
buryport. — See *Diplomatic Correspondence of the Revolution;* vol. I., p. 53.

† I have seen the despatch of the Marquis of Grimaldi to Count Aranda,
enclosing this draft for a million francs.

given that three thousand barrels of powder stored at New Orleans were at our service ;* the port of Havana was opened to us on the same terms as to

---

* The despatches of Oliver Pollock, the agent of Congress at New Orleans during the war, which are in the archives of the Department of State at Washington, throw the fullest light upon what was done by the Spanish Government in Louisiana.

As early as August, 1776, a cargo of powder was given by Governor Unzaga, despatched by Pollock, and arrived in safety. In January, 1777, Don Bernardo de Galvez succeeded Unzaga as governor. "That worthy nobleman," writes Pollock, "immediately made a tender of his services, and gave me the delightful assurance that he would go every possible length for the interest of Congress. I should be guilty of injustice, did I not declare that this generous promise was honorably fulfilled ; and I should belie my own heart if I did not on this, as on every other proper occasion, express my grateful sense of the services he has rendered to the United States. The first instance of them was retaliating the seizure of an American schooner in the lakes, by the seizure and confiscation of all British vessels between the Balize and Manchac, ... and by an assurance that the port of New Orleans should be open and free to American commerce, and to the admission and sale of prizes made by their cruisers."

Pollock not only sent military stores presented to Congress by the Spanish governor, but also made purchases of supplies amounting to $65,814, for the State of Virginia, and sent them by batteaux to different points on the Ohio. His drafts, authorized by Governor Patrick Henry, came back protested, placing him in the greatest embarrassment, from which he was generously relieved by Don Bernardo de Ottero, the Spanish Treasurer of Louisiana.

The course of events at New Orleans, under the brilliant young governor, Bernardo de Galvez, whose name a city of the United States now bears, is described in papers in the *Archivias de las Indias*, and has more than the interest of romance. A somewhat tardy recognition of his aid to us is found in a despatch written by order of Congress on the 21st November, 1781. This despatch, signed by Robert Morris, addressed to General Don Bernardo de Galvez, says :

"I am directed by the United States to express to your Excellency the grateful sense they entertain of your early efforts in their favor. Those generous efforts gave them so favorable an impression of your character and that of your nation, that they have not ceased to wish for an intimate connexion with your country."

France, and the further hint given that if an American ship should look in there occasionally it would find the door of a certain magazine open, and something in it useful to the Colonies.

Nor was this the end of Spanish favors. Blankets for ten regiments were sent as a present to Congress, through John Langdon, of Portsmouth; ship loads of stores were despatched through the house of Gardoqui, at Bilbao; and when John Jay appeared at Madrid as Minister of the new States, without any provision being made by Congress for money to pay even his house rent, another gift of $150,000 was made to him for us.

More yet. Though the declaration in regard to Capt. Lee was the earliest act of recognition by any power except France, Spain abstained from making a treaty with our Minister, for the very excellent reason that to do so would have been tantamount to a declaration of war against England, for which she was not prepared. But that eminent man who, on the 19th February, 1777, took the reins of power in Spain, Florida Blanca, was not idle. He immediately commenced building new ships and arming those already built — the annual expenses of the navy, usually about one hundred million reals, or five million dollars, were suddenly raised to twenty million dollars — and, in the spring of '79, thirty-six ships of the line, mounting more guns than any fleet she ever had, being ready for sea, she declared war against England. This immense fleet, of which seven were three-deckers, of 100 to 120 guns, (our solitary three-decker, the Pennsylvania, has never yet got to sea), this immense fleet joined the French fleet, sailed to attack the common enemy, and during that and the succeeding year intercepted the troops and supplies which had been sent to aid in our conquest.

Florida Blanca did not stop here, but, while engaged in his naval preparations, made a treaty with the Emperor of Morocco which closed his ports to the English. He also opened relations with Hyder Ali in India, and fomented the war which that powerful prince maintained against England. Benjamin Rush, writing shortly after to General Gates, says, "Heaven prosper our allies! Hyder Ali is the standing toast at my table." Florida Blanca did not rest content with this, but used all the wiles of diplomacy and all the force of Spain, to make difficulties for England in every part of the globe. When we are disposed to stretch the hand of covetousness toward any possession of now weakened Spain, let us remember the helping hand she gave to us in our hour of suffering and of peril.

But the labors of Spain did not end with this. England, driven to desperation, used all her arts to draw the northern powers into her alliance, and with Russia succeeded so well that orders were issued to fit out fifteen ships of the line at Cronstadt, and the intimation was given by the Empress Catharine to Sir James Harris, afterwards Lord Malmesbury, that this fleet would soon be ready to aid England in her contest.* British Ministers announced the joyful fact, and one of their journals, even before the ice was open in the Baltic, declared that the Russian fleet had already arrived at Plymouth.

In one week all this was changed; and there suddenly appeared in the spring of 1780, the important declaration of Russia that led to the armed neutrality, which has been called by writers on inter-

---

* On the 5th Nov., 1779, George III. wrote to the Empress Catharine: "The lively interest which you take in all that concerns Great Britain demands my thanks. In this, as on so many other occasions, I have admired the greatness of your talents, the extent of your knowledge, and the nobility of your sentiments. . . The designs of my enemies will not escape your penetration. . . . The use, or the simple show, of a part of your naval force, would restore and assure the repose of all Europe by dissipating the league which is formed against me."

On the 11th January, 1780, "another sop," (to use the language of the third Earl Malmesbury, in vol. I., p. 269, of his grandfather's writings,) " was given to the empress." On the 19th January, Sir James Harris handed to Prince Potemkin a memoir, written to show that, should the allies prevail against England, America would supply France with hemp, pitch, timber, &c., to the detriment of Russian trade.

" On the 22d February, 1780," says Harris, " Prince Potemkin sent for me, and with an impetuous joy, said, ' I heartily congratulate you; orders will be given to arm fifteen ships of the line and five frigates; they are to put to sea early in the spring. . . . It is entirely owing to what you have advanced. . . . Your nation may consider themselves as having twenty ships added to their fleet. . . . I am just come from the empress; it is by her particular orders I tell it to you.' He ended by desiring me to despatch my messenger immediately, expressing his impatience for this event being known in London." — Malmesbury; *Diaries and Correspondence*, I., 279.

national law, "the charter of the liberty of the
seas." By this, the empress declared that her fleet
was fitted out, not to aid England, but to maintain
the principles, that free ships make free goods—
that the neutral flag covers enemies' property—and
that no blockade which was not maintained by an
effective force, no blockade made merely by the
London Gazette, would be recognized as valid.

John Adams, then Minister at the Hague, saw at
once the whole force of this step, and, in a despatch
to Congress, said: "A declaration of war against England, on the part of Russia, could not have been
more decisive,"—and again, "the pretended preëm-
inence of the British flag is now destroyed." "Russia now will never take part with England, and all
the maritime powers must either remain neutral or
join against her."

In the House of Lords a wail of despair was
set up. "I shudder," said the Earl of Shelburne,
"when I think of this Russian manifesto; by it the
independence of America is consummated;" * and

---

* "The doctrine," said Earl Shelburne, " of ' free ships, free goods' at
once destroyed the law of nations as it had remained for many centuries;
but that was not all; it must terminate in the ruin of Britain, at least in the
overthrow of her naval power. . . . If France and Spain could trans-
port their property to and from the western world in free because neutral
bottoms, it was to the last degree ridiculous to say or believe that Great
Britain could possibly be able to cope with the united force of the House of
Bourbon. . . . Then farewell for ever to the naval power and glory of
Great Britain!"— *Parliamentary History*, XXI., 629 et seq.

Lord Camden declared that "the queen of the seas was deposed, and her sceptre fallen!"

Desperate efforts were made by British Ministers to meet the emergency. Appeals were addressed to Denmark and Sweden, but without effect; and, during this year, 1780, Sweden, Denmark and Holland joined in the league with Russia, which was in its effects a league of hostility to England. Holland also soon joined in the war; so that on one side stood England unaided and alone,— on the other, using all their forces against her, the United States, France, Spain, Hyder Ali, Holland; while all the northern powers were armed, nominally neutral, but really hostile to her autocratic pretensions.

One of our wisest statesmen, John Adams, exclaimed a few years later: "We owe the blessings of peace not to the causes assigned, but to the armed neutrality." And who was the real author of the armed neutrality? Who conceived that act, and who, by his ingenuity and indefatigable perseverance, led Russia and with her the northern powers to adopt it?—Florida Blanca, the Minister of Spain. And to him and to his country, I here render the honor, with all the more pleasure that this has not usually been done, and that the documents which establish their claim to it are in my possession.

For such aid as the armed neutrality gave us— again we have to thank Spain.

With all this inequality of force the war still went on. Constant efforts were made by England to induce the Colonies to return to their allegiance; and, to their shame be it said, men were found ready to listen to her propositions; men who seduced by the hope of rewards, and by the promise of office for themselves or for their sons, consented to sneer at and to deny the principles of the Declaration. It was after intercourse with such men, that the intelligent agent of one of our allies wrote home to his government that there was more real enthusiasm for American liberty in the smallest *café* in Paris, than in a large portion of the society which he met.

Again and again were terms offered by England to Spain and to France, but the constant reply was, a refusal to treat until we were free.

Peace and freedom were at length secured; and from that time, through various vicissitudes and difficulties, our country, — by confidence in democratic principles, by faith in the people, and by the spirit of mutual forbearance and charity among them, — has gone on prospering and increasing, till in *material* force it stands among the mightiest; and, did we but always act up to the immortal truths of the Declaration, would, in *moral* force, be the mightiest of the earth.

While the old world, to which we turned for succor against our unnatural parent, is echoing to the
clang of arms, and hostile legions stand arrayed for
combat,

> " We may live securely in our towns ;
>   We may sit
> Under our vines and make the miseries
> Of other nations a discourse for us,
> And lend them sorrows ; — for ourselves, we may
> Safely forget there are such things as tears."

But it is not in man to be indifferent. The en-
during sympathies of our nature demand an object;
and besides, our early ties to France must make us
feel a special interest in her actions and destiny.
What, then, is the object of the war in which she is
engaged, and what responsibility have we in the contest?

The actual war between Italy and France on one
side, and Austria on the other, is but the continua-
tion of our own struggle on another field — the struggle for independence, equal rights and self-government. How far these may be secured by the present
contest is very uncertain ; but there is no uncertainty
in this, that our warmest sympathies are due to all
who strive for them.

In the present case these sympathies are augmented
by a remembrance of all we owe to Italy — that
beautiful country which the Apennines divide, the

Alps and sea surround — Italy, which has given us so much of all that adorns and elevates life; the home of art, of science, of medical skill, of political knowledge; of Galileo, Raffael, Michael Angelo, of Fallopio and of Volta; the land which in modern times has given us the earliest epic poet, Dante; the great lyric poets, Petrarch and Filicaia; the earliest novelist, Boccacio; the first philosophical historian, Machiavelli; and the founder of the philosophy of history, Vico, whose great mind has brought to the development of political science and the laws of the moral world the same precision that Galileo had brought to those of the material world.

To Italy we owe the mariner's compass, the barometer, book-keeping, the telescope applied to astronomy, the calculation of longitudes, the pendulum as a measure of time, the laws of hydraulics, the rules of navigation: and to Italy we owe both Columbus, who discovered, and Amerigo Vespucci, who gave his name to our country.

To Italy we owe also some of the most important lessons of political philosophy. Her Republics of the middle ages were based on the three great principles:

1st. That all authority over the people emanates from the people.

2d. That power should return at stated intervals to the people.

3d. That the holder of power should be strictly *responsible to the people* for its use.*

To those Republics we also owe the practical demonstration of the great truth, that no State can long prosper or exist where intelligent labor is not held in honor, and that labor cannot be honorable where it is not free.

Our sympathies are augmented by a remembrance of all this, and by the natural horror inspired by Austria — to whom civilization for three hundred and thirty years owes nothing, — whose whole career, both at home and abroad, has been a series of blackest crimes against the political rights of States, and the individual rights of man, — and who is now under the despotic control of an emperor, himself a deplorable example of the union of youth and cruelty.

But there are some, happily their number is small, who, having no faith in the people, look with indifference upon their efforts, — and others who try to cloak the selfishness and imbecility with which nature has endowed them, under an assumed superiority over the people of other countries, — who tell us that

---

* "The whole system of Italian liberty is represented in these three axioms. In fact, the Italian republics were freer than those of Germany, than the imperial and Hanseatic cities, than the Swiss Cantons, than the United Provinces, perhaps even than the republics of antiquity. All these had sought, not the security, but the sovereignty of the citizens; not to protect the citizen against the government, but to create a government to the power of which, with a blind and unlimited confidence, they neglected to fix any bounds." — Sismondi, *Histoire des Républiques Italiennes,* XVI., 394.

other nations are not fitted for free institutions, — who seem to think that they have a patent for freedom, and an exclusive right to enjoy it, — that they are God's chosen people, and that all others are made only to be ruled by tyrants.

Others, again, who have a sense of natural right, and common sense besides, but whose natures are not hopeful, point to the example of France, and in her failures to maintain a stable republican government, find, as they imagine, the justification of all their misgivings. As the events now passing in Italy must produce a recoil in France, and as the power of self-government in Italians will by some be judged of by that exhibited by the French, it may be well to look for a moment at this.

It is only stating what many wise French writers have admitted, that their Revolution of 1789 was brought on by our own. Before '76, the labors of Fenelon, Montesquieu, Turgot, and other French philosophers, had developed ideas upon the rights of man, and the science of government, which, to this day, stand as the landmarks of an advancing civilization. They had all asserted the natural rights of man, and all recognized that nations had rights flowing directly from these, and not drawn from old charters or from musty parchments. With this there was, on their part, a large and generous appreciation of the relations which should subsist between different countries.

Montesquieu had laid down the proposition, for which he is sharply attacked by Lord Brougham, that " the whole system of international law is a set of obvious corollaries to a maxim in ethics — that in war nations should do as little injury, and in peace as much good to each other, as is consistent with their individual safety."

Turgot, the great statesman, whose Latin inscription for a memorial of Franklin* has been adopted by the city of Boston — and who may be called the father of free-trade — Turgot had labored for three great objects :

1st. To check religious intolerance.

2d. To reduce, and finally suppress, standing armies.

3d. To establish free trade.

And the whole political code of this hard-headed, practical statesman and successful financier, may be summed up in his declaration that " when called upon to decide if any measure were useful for France, the

---

* Turgot's first inscription was in French verse :

Le voilà ce mortel dont l'heureuse industrie,
Sut enchaîner la Foudre et lui donner des loix,
Dont la sagesse active et l'éloquente voix,
D'un pouvoir oppresseur affranchit sa Patrie,
Qui désarma les Dieux, qui réprime les Rois.

Which, subsequently, he condensed into this admirable line :

Eripuit Cœlo fulmen, sceptrumque Tyrannis.

Oeuvres de Turgot, IX., 140.

question must first be asked, *Is it useful for all man-kind?* for whatever temporary advantage may appear to accrue from acting on a different principle, nothing in the long run can be good for one nation which is not good for all."

These philosophers turned their eyes toward England, as then offering the only example in the world of a certain degree of liberty; this they recognized in the independence of her judiciary and in the grand principles — fortunately our heritage — which guided it. The words of Algernon Sidney were familiar to them: "Common sense declares that governments are instituted, and judicatures erected, for the obtaining of justice. The king's bench was not established that the chief justice should have a great office, but that the oppressed should be relieved, and right done. The honor and profit he receives, come as the rewards of his service, if he rightly perform his duty." And again: "The power with which the judges are entrusted is but of a moderate extent, and to be executed *bona fide.* Prevarications are capital, as they proved to Tresilian, Empson, Dudley, and many others." *

No passage from Sidney was more frequently referred to than this: "They who uphold the rightful power of a just magistracy, encourage virtue and

* Sidney; *Discourses on Government,* chap. iii, sec. 26.

justice; teach men what they ought to do, suffer, or expect from others; fix them upon principles of honesty; and generally advance everything that tends to the increase of the valor, strength, greatness and happiness of the nation, creating a good union among them, and bringing every man to an exact understanding of his own and the public rights. On the other side, he that would introduce an ill magistrate, make one evil who was good, or preserve him in the exercise of injustice when he is corrupted, must always open the way for him by vitiating the people, corrupting their manners, destroying the validity of oaths and contracts, teaching such evasions, equivocations and frauds, as are inconsistent with the thoughts that become men of virtue and courage."* The declaration of Chief Justice Lee was also cited by them with admiration — "One rule can never vary in our courts, viz., the Eternal rule of Natural Justice."†

Montesquieu had shown in his great work that the separation of powers, judicial, executive and legislative, was the basis of all free government; and, acting upon this, much had been done, even before '89, to improve the administration of justice.

---

* *Ibid*, chap. iii, sec. 20 : III. 129. Edit. 1805.

† These words of C. J. Lee will be found in the case of *Omychund* v. *Barker*, Atkyns's Reports, I. 46.

The Constitution of '89 gave to France self-government, and recognized the sovereignty of the people. No honest man had anything to fear from this Constitution, but all who lived by oppression and wrong were filled with dismay. The Christian doctrines of Turgot and Montesquieu, and the principle that governments were made for men, and not men for governments, shook the despotic thrones to their base. Their trembling occupants conspired at Mantua and Pilnitz, and formed a league to crush the constitutional government of France.

In August, 1792, the armies of despotism arrived on the frontier, threatening to overturn that government, and, if opposed, to reduce Paris to ashes. Then, in the fear and frenzy which ensued, began those acts of violence which have left a stain upon the French Revolution. "Nothing," says one of the most conservative writers upon international policy, "can ever justify one State's interfering with the internal affairs of another; and the worst of mischiefs (the execution of those who have aided it) must ever be the result of such interference;" and it is to this infamous and unprovoked attempt to interfere by arms with the internal affairs of France, that we must trace the death of Louis XVI., and all the violence and all the difficulties which followed it.

France had done nothing to provoke interference;

and, left to herself, might and probably would have organized and sustained a good government. This assertion I boldly make, conscious that it does not accord with what some of us have been taught. The enemies of liberty have not scrupled on every occasion to distort the truth, and have even on one occasion found an accidental ally in a President of the United States.

Mr. Millard Fillmore, in the last annual message he sent to Congress, says that France showed a desire to force her form of government upon all the world, and points to a decree of her Convention, declaring she was ready to succor oppressed nations struggling for liberty, as the false step which brought against her the coalitions and armies of Europe. Had Mr. Fillmore but looked at the facts, he would have found that the provocation to hostilities came not from France, but from the despotic confederates; and that the decree in question, at the same time that it showed a generous spirit, was also a measure of self-defence. The Convention of Mantua was signed 20th May, 1791; that of Pilnitz the 29th August, 1791; and it was not until the 19th November, 1792, after the actual invasion of France, and eighteen months after the first coalition against her, that the Convention voted the decree which President Fillmore leads us to infer was the cause of that invasion and of that coalition; the cause, in presidential logic, coming eighteen months after the effect.*

But there are too many who speak of France, not with any accurate knowledge of facts, but with reckless assertion, and a seemingly wilful blindness to truth and to principle.

This is not the place for long dissertations, but a candid examination of facts will show that the French people have never yet had a fair chance. From 1792 to 1830, the prolonged pressure upon France of despotic Europe, under the lead for a long time of England, prevented her from forming a good government. The revolution of 1830 secured the rights of only 240,000; the thirty-six millions of Frenchmen being declared by Guizot to be no part of the "lawful country."† The revolution of 1848 made of these outlaws citizens, and they marked their possession of power by securing to France three thousand new school houses — by giving her cheap postage — by making all bondmen in her colonies free—and by placing for two years her budget in equilibrium. During the eighteen years of Louis Philippe's reign the

---

* A statement of Lord Brougham has led many persons into this same historical error. "The famous decree of 19th November, 1792, was a main cause of the dreadful war which so long laid Europe waste, and overthrew so many established governments." — *Brougham* VIII., 79. But the invasion of France took place some time before this decree.

† "*Je ne connais que le pays légal.*" Guizot — Speech in the Chamber of Deputies.

expenses had been every year fifty million dollars more than the receipts, while under Louis Napoleon the annual deficit has been upwards of one hundred million dollars. To the Republican government of 1848 belongs the exclusive honor of having, for two years, kept its cash account square.

This government fell, through the perjury of an usurper, and through the passive obedience of a standing army — an army which despotic coalitions had taught France to regard as necessary for her safety.

Before we revile the French people for having permitted this usurpation, let us remember that it was not accomplished without a bloody resistance, and that the people in the provinces showed the spirit of self-government which was in them, by refusing for a long time to submit to the dictation of the capital.

Let us remember also that our own Congress, sitting in Philadelphia, was in 1783 assailed by armed invaders of its Hall, and took refuge in another city.

Let us again remember that on this very day, three years ago, an assembly of the people in a territory of the United States, peacefully discussing the formation of their institutions, was dispersed by the bayonets of the Federal army.

One of the most acute and learned of living American publicists — worthy son of worthy sires — Mr. Charles Francis Adams, in the admirable notes to the writings of his grandfather, suggests the single legislative assembly as one great cause of the want of stability of Republican forms in France ; and, in regard to the Italian Republics of the middle ages, he alludes to the absence of a respect for the rights of the minority as one of the latent causes of their downfall. This same observation upon the minority has been applied by others to France.

It may not, perhaps, be generally known that the adoption of a single chamber in France was due, in a great degree, to the labors of our own philosopher and statesman, Franklin. As President of the State Convention of Pennsylvania, he had secured the adoption in their constitution of a single chamber—in his writings he had praised it — and the Committee of the French National Assembly, La Rochefoucauld, Sieyes, Mirabeau and others, give to Franklin the honor of having aided them, as they say, " to clear the legislative machine of its multiplied movements and much praised balances, which made it only complicated and cumbersome ; " and this opinion of Franklin was also relied upon in the adoption of the Republican Constitution of 1848. While admitting the error in this, we may surely pardon something to those who have been led astray by faith in our own great men.

In regard to the rights of minorities, every revolution in France has shown an increasing respect for them on the part of the people ; and in the most violent popular clubs of 1848, were heard words like these : " We ask no exclusive legislation for ourselves; on the contrary, let us remember always to guard the rights of the minority ; as the law of civilized States throws its tutelary protection with special force over minors and wards, so let us, being in power, remember that the defeated minority are our wards, and that we are their responsible guardians." Compared with a sentiment of high and generous statesmanship like this, coming to us though it do from a " red-repub- lican " club in Paris, what an ignoble contrast is pre- sented by that cry of demagogues — that Indian war- whoop of party leaders — " to the victor belong the spoils."

Under all recent governments in France, the spirit of inquiry in her people has remained ever active, and the character of her judiciary generally unspotted. The reply of President Séguier to an improper de- mand of power will be recalled : " The court renders judgments, not favors." Under the first Napoleon, some of the courts, it is true, degenerated; but the Paris bar has punished, by remembering, the judge whose often repeated formula was : *L'empereur a dit, et je vous le répéte* — " the emperor has said, and I repeat it " — and one of the declared reasons for the overthrow of Napoleon was, that he had " confounded all powers, and destroyed the independence of the judiciary." *

* See the *Senatus Consultum* of April, 1814, Sec. VII.

5

Every change in France has shown a higher development, a larger education, and a greater power of self-government on the part of her people. It has taken England some six hundred years to bring her parliamentary machine into its actual state; and yet, only four years ago, the husband of Queen Victoria publicly stated, at the Trinity House dinner, that it must be regarded as still on trial. Let us not, then, question the capacity of the French, or the Italian, or the German people, simply because they may fail to achieve in six months what England has worked upon for six centuries.

But, we are told that Italy will only change its master, and that France will take the place of Austria. It is not the interest of Louis Napoleon to remain in Italy, nor is it possible, under any circumstances, for France to degrade herself to the level of Austria.

The career of the elder Napoleon in Italy, which was such as to cause his name to be still revered there, may here be safely appealed to. Industry was awakened and encouraged, schools founded, the sciences stimulated, and academies organized by him who had destroyed them in Paris. The courts were changed, and in place of a system which favored and even required servile and corrupt judges, one was installed which led to the impartial administration of justice. The armies of France, under Napoleon, brought to Italy some of the fruits of the revolution of '89. If the worst predictions of the enemies of the war should be fulfilled, and Italy gain by it only a French master, it would still, judging by the past, be a change from darkness to light, from a government of the most loathsome brutality to one of comparative civilization.

And here let me say, that if I seem to speak harshly of the Austrian domination in Italy, it is because, with my own eyes, I have seen its effects. I will not sadden this day by the recital of atrocities, the remembrance of which, even at this distance, chills my blood. To me it seems incredible that any one can be found ready to defend the government which practises them.

Nor has Italy received anything from Austria in exchange for all her sufferings. The well-made roads, which are pointed out to the stranger, were nearly all the work of Italian engineers during the time of Napoleon; but even if some material improvement had been made, it would be as nothing compared to the immense amounts Austria has drawn from Lombardy, by forced loans and by crushing taxation. About fifty per cent. of the revenue of land-owners goes to the Austrian treasury; "and all we get in exchange," said a Lombard to me, "is, once a week, the music of an Austrian regiment."

But give Italy a fair chance. Take from her the
incubus of Austria. Take away those bayonets, with
which, through a blind reverence on the part of
other States, for existing abuses and the balance of
power, Austria has been allowed to transpierce her.
"Let the thief and the receiver, the murderer and
the robber be no longer suffered to play the part of
watchmen" in Europe, and no one can doubt the
result for Italy.

It does not follow that a perfectly balanced government will leap at once into life. Difficulties of
internal organization doubtless will arise. Mazzini
will strive for a united, central republic, while others
will be glad to place themselves under the constitutional system, which has developed statesmen like
Cavour and Azeglio, to plan their wars and alliances,
and brave captains like Victor Emanuel, to lead
their armies. These differences of opinion will create discussion, into which, perhaps, excited feeling
will sometimes enter; our own conventions will have
set them the example; but to all prophets of evil
it is sufficient to say, that the Italian people have
the perfect right to judge of their own institutions,
and if they find pleasure in it, to wrangle over them.
They may, perhaps, think that nothing is so good
as the jar of a constitutional discussion to shake up
the stagnant elements of a slumbering society. Looking from a distance, if we might venture to express

desires upon a matter which exclusively concerns the Italian people themselves, it would be that, with some changes in the actual boundaries of States, representative institutions, securing the largest liberty, should be founded in each of them, and a central federative government be created to administer such powers as the several States should confide to it.

The "United States of Italy" thus formed would satisfy the love of unity, so strong in the Italian heart, while the State organization would give full play to that spirit of local and municipal liberty, which, in former days, was so fully developed in the Italian Republics.

The great work of this war would however be very imperfectly done, if it stopped with the liberation of Italy. Already in 1848, the unaided Italians having taken Peschiera, and driven Austria behind the walls of Verona and Mantua, which, for some time to come, will probably be her stronghold, she offered to treat with France and England as mediators for the surrender of Lombardy, provided the new State would assume a portion of her enormous debt.

If nothing be done now but to rescue Italy, and peace be then made with Austria, that peace can be only a truce; for we may expect, in a short time, to see her return to her old course, and again, by her outrages, disturb the civilization of the world.

After Italy is secured to freedom, there still remains Hungary.

This country, whose constitution goes back almost to the date of Magna Charta, and which had preserved its political independence, though exposed to every species of encroachment from the Austrian archdukes, whom, in an evil hour, it had invited to its throne; this country, so brave and so unfortunate, merits all our interest, for it is the home of heroes, and of self-sacrificing, honorable men.

Some five and twenty years ago, several Hungarian noblemen visited the United States, travelled throughout the country, and had the good fortune in Boston to form an intimacy with a gentleman whose views upon European questions were as enlightened as his general knowledge was varied and profound — Mr. Alexander H. Everett. On their return to Hungary, one of their number, Farkas Sandor, published, in the Magyar tongue, a book pointing out the working of our institutions; and, in which while rendering thanks to Mr. Everett for the counsels received, he recommended the policy of the Northern States as an example for Hungary. The German translation of this work was prohibited by Austria, but the Hun-

garian edition had already gone beyond the reach
of her police. The effect of the excursion to America was soon apparent. At the next session of the
Diet, Baron Wesselenyi, Count Bathjany, and others
of the travellers and their friends, proposed a series
of measures tending to the abolition of those feudal
privileges which divided the Hungarian people into
hostile classes, and offered at once to lay down
their titles and their power for the common good.

Austria now took the alarm. She had always pretended to be the friend of the peasants against the
nobles, — but when the nobles proposed to give up
their privileges and emancipate the serfs, she then
used all her power to oppose them. There was a
deep and wicked policy in this; it being the aim of
Austria to keep up such a hostility between classes,
such a war between capital and labor, that she might
be able at some time completely to subjugate Hungary, by calling upon the peasants to cut the throats
of the land-owners. And this, in the spring of 1846,
she actually did, in the neighboring province of
Galicia.

Shortly after, two men appeared upon the scene,
Count Stephen Sechenyi and Louis Kossuth. Sechenyi sought the advancement of Hungary through
material improvements; Kossuth sought it through
the education of the people, and by awakening in
the minds of the more fortunate classes of society

a sense of their duties. By securing to the peasants the right of voting for a delegate to represent their villages at the general election,— thus
bringing home to them the practice of free institutions, without, however, creating such a mass of
new voters as would suddenly disturb the general
result,— by settling the eternal question of capital
and labor, and making the holders of each clearly
understand that their real interests are reciprocal;
by these and kindred measures — which prepared
the way for that larger liberty secured to all classes
during the constitutional ministry of Kossuth — that
eminent orator and tribune showed himself in Hungary to be a great, practical, conservative statesman.

The Emperor of Austria having called in foreign
troops to put down the legal government of Hungary, and having neglected to take the oath of
allegiance to her Constitution, which the compact
between the Hungarian nation and the Dukes of
Austria made the indispensable preliminary to any
act of sovereignty on his part, the Diet, in the
name of the people of Hungary, on the anniversary
of the battle of Lexington, 1849, declared that all
connection between them and the house of Austria
was dissolved.

The noble struggle made by the Hungarian people is still fresh in your memories. The forces of
despotism were too strong, and their country fell.

Had any other State recognized their independence, it would have enabled them to contract a loan, and to purchase the arms necessary for the contest. Our own Congress was unable to contract any loan until our independence had been recognized in Europe. To the eternal honor of Mr. Clayton, then Secretary of State, a commissioner was despatched with full powers to enter into negotiations with the new government; but he, alas! arrived too late.

England looked calmly on while a government similar to her own was destroyed by foreign arms. Had she, in the summer of 1849, opened relations with the constitutional government of Hungary, which she could have done without shaking any existing right; without even giving any just cause of disturbance to "those finical personages who," in the words of an English peer, himself a negotiator, "have brought a sort of ridicule upon the name of diplomacy;" had she then taken her stand upon the Pragmatic Sanction of 1723, and upon the coronation oath of the last king — both which documents, duly filed away in red tape at the foreign office, make part of the public law of Europe, and by both which the Austrian sovereigns recognize the political independence of Hungary — had she done this, she might have spared herself all the sacrifices of her war in the Crimea, and all the embarrassments of the present contest.

Then there might have been at the present moment a great Constitutional State, on the banks of the Danube, having municipal institutions which secured local rights, and a population accustomed to constitutional forms, and to liberty founded on law. Here would have been a nucleus round which the different provinces of Turkey might have clustered, as they dropped away from her corrupt body; and Hungary, Transylvania, Valachia, Moldavia, Servia, Bosnia, and Bulgaria have formed the " United States of the Danube," — a grateful and efficient ally for England. But the blind admiration for Austria on the part of the English aristocracy, strengthened by the labors of Metternich, then in London, would not permit this recognition.

" Of all the subjects which can come before the people at large," says Lord Brougham, in one of his political essays, " the foreign policy of the State is the one on which they the least deserve to be consulted. Their interests are most materially affected by it, no doubt, for on it depends the great question of peace or war. But the bearing upon their interests of any particular operation is far from being immediate, and a measure may be most necessary for securing the peace, even the independence of the nation, and yet its connexion with these great objects be far too remote for the popular eye to reach it." *

* This was written in 1843. See Brougham's *Works*, VIII., 93.

The events of the year 1849 in England, offer
a singular commentary upon this dogma of Lord
Brougham. Then the *people* saw clearly the interest of England; the ruling classes did not. The
people flooded the House of Commons with petitions
for the recognition of Hungarian Independence; the
aristocracy remained idle. A few like Lord Lynd-
hurst, the Marquis of Northampton, and the lamented
Earl Fitzwilliam were true to themselves, and acted
like enlightened English noblemen, but the greater
part stood in cold indifference to Hungary, or joined
the sharers in Metternich's Eaton-Square dinners
in looking with delight at the triumph of her enemy

And what is this Austrian empire, in sympathy
for which the ruling classes of England forget the
interests of their country and the interests of humanity? An agglomeration of States, differing in
nationality, language and religion, brought together
by fraud and violence, and held by brute force, in
subjection to a government the most infamous in
history.

Bohemia, the land of John Huss and Jerome of
Prague, was annexed after a series of atrocities which
make the Spanish Inquisition appear respectable in
our eyes. Three million inhabitants were reduced
to seven hundred and eighty thousand, and of thirty
thousand seven hundred villages, only six thousand
were left standing.

Excepting the Tyrol, the same atrocities, though in less degree, have been practised in every one of the different States;—the forces drawn from all being used against any one which showed a spark of liberty. As a general rule, the soldiers of each State have been sent to distant provinces, of the language of which they were ignorant, and where there was little probability that any relations would spring up to weaken the blind submission imposed on them by military servitude. Sometimes, as in the recent battles in Italy, the young soldiers, torn by her conscription from the soil, have been placed by Austria in the front rank, and fired upon from behind, if they shrank from slaying their friends and deliverers.

The government of this empire has, when in danger, constantly promised reforms in the provinces, and as steadily opposed reforms when the danger was passed. Its permanent policy has been to keep up a state of endless hostility between classes; to rule by dividing, by making appeals to the most anarchical passions, by exciting to plunder, and even, as in Galicia, to assassination.

This government is not an aristocracy of virtue, of talent, of birth nor of wealth, but of soldiers and bureaucrats; whose practice on many occasions has been the development of the principles of the most exaggerated communism. Property has not been respected by them any more than liberty;—whenever the treasury was empty, it has had no rights sacred in their eyes.

The Austrian government has not scrupled, over and over again, to repudiate a large portion of its national debt, to cut down to one-half their nominal value its treasury notes, and to collect forced loans. All Europe would have rung with indignation had any of these deeds been done by a liberal government. The culminating outrage, however, of Austria upon the rights of property was perpetrated in 1852, when the emperor, proclaiming himself the guardian of all minor orphans, dispossessed the rightful guardians and trustees, seized upon four hundred and seventy million dollars — the heritage of the fatherless — and gave in exchange his own promises to pay.

The personal violence committed, even in the old German provinces, would seem almost incredible to one who had not himself witnessed it. The printed law prohibits the flogging of women. The governor of one of the provinces, with whom I happened to be well acquainted, pointed out to me this law, which he had shown a few days before to an English noble-man who admired Austria. "Here," said the governor, showing me the law, "is the *text*, and here," handing me reports from the police, describing the flogging of two women that very morning, "*here is the sermon.*"

One of the greatest sticklers for existing States, and upholders of the actual balance of power, Lord

Brougham, speaking of the partition of Poland, has said, "It would not be easy to see any danger arising to the North American Union from that partition in 1793-4, or the Holy Alliance in 1816 and 1820; and yet it is certain that the Americans had a right to complain of such acts being permitted, because the impunity of the wrong-doers gave a blow to the political morality of all nations, and lowered the tone of public principle. The United States were interested like all other countries, in seeing that the principle of National Independence was held sacred, that none could conspire against it with impunity." *

If this be true, then certainly we have a right to protest against the conduct of Austria, which is a prolonged violation of the principles of national independence, and of political and private morality; and since it is now clear that it is only by this conduct that she lives and moves and has her being — that her existence hangs upon injustice and outrage — then, following up the reasoning of our statesman, so conservative on questions of foreign policy, we have a right to protest against the very existence of the Austrian empire.

Civilization and humanity demand that this wretched machine of cruelty should be broken up; that this opprobrium of the nineteenth century and of the

* Essay on General Principles of Foreign Policy. Brougham's *Works.* VIII., 76.

human race should be resolved into its elements — and the so-called emperor, with the German provinces, take his place, an humble archduke, in the German Confederation.

Then might Galicia and Bohemia resume their position with the Slavonic family; then would Hungary become again free; and then Germany, no longer having Austria to crush her, as in 1850, with the forces of States foreign to her, might awaken to a new life, and found a government in which liberty and order should be secured by making the German people interested in their maintenance; a government in which her men of science should take their true position, which should not condemn to death her poets, nor cause her historians to pine in dungeons * — which should not force her Humboldts to vote with the opposition, nor drive her Bunsens into political exile. Then might there be peace, and not merely a truce in Europe; and the beneficent plans of Turgot for reducing standing armies be carried out.

But the great obstacle to this happy consummation is the policy which the ruling classes in England impose upon her government. The crimes of Austria may be traced directly home to England, as without the moral support of that power she could not stand a twelvemonth. The traditions of the foreign office,

---

* As was the case in 1850 with the poet Kinkel, and with the Professor of History in the Heidelberg University, Gervinus.

and of the governing classes, based on the events of a hundred and fifty years ago, point to the house of Austria as the necessary ally of England. Scarce one of the conditions which then led to that alliance exists now. Thus it is ever with European policy. Men of genius conceive a system appropriate for a given series of facts; the facts change, but formalists, unable to appreciate the *motive* of the system, move on in the old track to their own perdition.

Knowing how completely her existence depended upon the favor of England, Austria has used all her wiles to retain it. Weak young Englishmen of family, attracted to Vienna by its cheap and facile vices, have been caressed and flattered. On the arrival of Englishmen of any political importance, immediate notice has been given by the police, and the hint conveyed to certain adherents of the crown to treat them with hospitality, and to twine Austrian corkscrews round their hearts.

She has also used her money successfully with a portion of the European press. Hence the blatant articles we have read upon a march to Paris. Attempts have even been made in this country, but, to the honor of the American press, no editor has been found willing to soil his hands with the money stolen from the orphans of Vienna.

On the great questions of the day the English *people* are perfectly sound, but the foreign policy of

England is directed by men who care but little for the popular sentiment; who decide questions neither by rules of natural right, nor by the dictates of a far-seeing statesmanship; and who, be they Tories or Whigs, have a devotion to Austria so blind and so infatuated, that it can only be disturbed by the fear of losing their places, or the fear of bringing upon England a great calamity.

And here begin our duties and our responsibilities. In whatever contest ensues, our sympathies should be with those who strive for their natural rights; with those who strive to imitate us in what we have done of good; and to them we owe all the aid we can give, without directly plunging into the contest.

No English ministry would rashly enter into a war, which promised to be long and complicated, without assuring and strengthening its friendly relations with the United States. This may now be regarded as a rule of English polity. Let us make the English government clearly understand that in no case, and in no form, can it have aid from us, in any measure tending to uphold the house of Austria. More, let us say to that government, that in such a course, she shall have, at all times — and in every manner, short of actual war, by which we can reach her — our determined hostility.

Let us do for the old world what the old world did

for us in our struggle for Independence. Let us, in favor of the right, interpose another "ARMED NEUTRALITY"— a neutrality armed, not with the cannon of Catharine, but with the printing press and the electric light of truth. And the mighty public opinion thus created, shall come to aid the English people in keeping their rulers in the path of duty, of justice, and of humanity.

But our responsibilities do not stop here. We owe it to those who look to us for a model, *we owe it to ourselves*, to give them an example of good government; of a government which at all times and in all places shall be true to the memories and to the principles of the day we celebrate; of a government free from corruption; and so well balanced as never to permit the encroachment of any one of the three great branches of power upon the legitimate field of another.

We have already seen that, even a century ago in France, the idea of civil liberty implied an independent, but rigidly responsible judiciary, and a complete separation of the legislative, executive and judicial functions.

It was an old rule of the Parliament of Paris that no member of that court should go to the Louvre, or frequent the houses of princes; and in England, without there being, as I believe, any positive rule, custom requires that the puisne judges shall never go to the Court of the Sovereign. This provision is one of many to keep the judiciary above even the suspicion of making itself an instrument for despotism in the hands of the executive.

In France, where the theory of institutions is more closely studied than in England, ample provision has been also made to prevent any usurpation by the judiciary of the functions of the legislature.

One of the most ingenious and profound of modern authors — Jules Simon — speaking of the progress in the development of judicial institutions, even in countries where but little progress has been made in other things, says: "If placed before judges a thousand miles from home, and called on to plead a cause, I know that if my cause be just, and my judges be honest, I shall win it; and this because the great principles which regulate the conduct of judges are everywhere the same."*

Of these great principles, one of the most important is that which confines the judge strictly to the case and point before him, which does not permit him to wander from that, and which forbids him, under any pretext, to make of the judicial bench a tripod or a stump.

* *Le Devoir, par* Jules Simon. Simon, like Arago, gave up lucrative places under the French government, rather than swear allegiance to a usurper. He has just been nominated to the chair in the Institute, made vacant by the death of de Tocqueville.

"An opinion," said Chief Justice Vaughan, "given in court, if not necessary to the judgment given of record, is *no* judicial opinion;"[*] and Chief Justice Willes says, "great mischiefs must arise from judges giving such opinions."[†]

The great legal minds of France have spoken with even more force. "The judge," say they, "is necessarily confined strictly to the point legally brought before him. If he permit himself, even with good intentions, to wander from this — to express from the bench opinions upon other matters — opinions which it is true would have no judicial value, but which might have an effect upon timid and ignorant minds — *he unfits himself for the office of a judge.* He throws away the impartiality which he should have when a point, similar to that which he has discoursed upon, comes lawfully before him; and he encroaches upon the first branch of the sovereign power — the legislative — all which is inadmissible in a well-organized society."[‡]

---

[*] *Bole* v. *Horton*, Vaughan's R. 382. "An extra-judicial opinion given in or out of court is no more than the prolatum or saying of him who gives it, nor can be taken as his opinion, unless everything spoken at pleasure must pass as the speaker's opinion."—*Ibid.*

[†] Willes, 666. See also Ram, *On Legal Judgment*, 22.

[‡] See the debates upon the adoption of the Code Napoléon for a full discussion of this interesting subject; also Berryat de Saint-Prix, *Cours de Procédure Civile;* and Meyer, *Origine et Progrés des Institutions Judiciaires en Europe.* This last authority, speaking of the courts of civilized states, says: "Penetrated with the truth that courts are established in order to bring dif-

In no country has the judiciary been more constantly respected than in our own. It has deserved respect, for it has respected itself. The decisions of Marshall, of Story, and of Curtis have been adopted as law, in the courts of other countries. The severe criticisms of Jefferson upon the Supreme Court of the United States have not generally been concurred in by the intelligent mind of the country. He charged that court with arrogance, and with having both the power and the will to overturn the constitutional liberties of the country.* Upon no point was the

ferences to an end; that their authority is based only on the requisition of parties who implore their aid; that, in one word, judges are made for pleaders, and not pleaders for judges; the legislator has laid down the principle that the judge can give no decision or opinion except upon the requisition of one of the parties to a suit, and in the limits fixed by that requisition. The judge is free to grant or to deny what is asked; to ask for further information without which he feels unable to decide; to allow a part only of what is asked; but he cannot exceed the demand made, neither in quantity nor in quality. . . . The judicial power is by its very nature *passive*. He who holds in his hands the balance of justice cannot lean to one side without causing it to incline. The judge who agitates, under whatever motive or pretext, cannot be impartial." — *Meyer;* IV., 527 *et seq.*

* Jefferson says, in 1820: "The judiciary of the United States is the subtle corps of sappers and miners constantly working underground to undermine the foundations of our confederated fabric. They are construing our Constitution from a co-ordination of a general and special government to a general and supreme one alone. This will lay all things at their feet. . . . Having found, from experience, that impeachment is an impracticable thing — a mere scarecrow — they consider themselves secure for life; they skulk from responsibility to public opinion, the only remaining hold on them. An opinion is huddled up in conclave, perhaps by a majority of one, delivered as if unanimous, and with the silent acquiescence of lazy or timid associates, by a crafty chief judge, who sophisticates the law to his mind by the turn of his own reasoning." — *Writings of Jefferson, published by order of Congress,* VII., 192. See also pp. 199, 216, 256, 278, 293, 321, 403.

great father of American democracy more earnest than upon this; and no opinion of his brought upon him more severe attacks from his political opponents.

Hamilton, in earlier days, and more recently the learned Justice Story, insisted on the other hand, that it would be difficult and almost impossible for the Supreme Court to go astray—that the cases upon which it could lawfully act were strictly limited,* and Story declared that, should it ever exceed its powers or make a wrong decision, the enlightened public opinion of the country, closely watching it, would recall it to a sense of duty.

A recent scene in the Supreme Court of the United States has at length justified the forebodings

---

* Hamilton's opinions upon the limited power of the Supreme Court as laid down in the *Federalist* are further developed in the 3d and 4th vols. of the *History of the Republic* by his son, John C. Hamilton. Story, in his *Commentaries on the Constitution,* §1777, 2d edition, says: "The functions of the judges of the courts of the United States are strictly and exclusively judicial. They cannot, therefore, be called upon to advise the president in any executive measures, or to give extra-judicial interpretations of law."

Some confusion exists in the popular mind from the often repeated assertion that it is the province of the Supreme Court to decide all constitutional *questions.* Story says: "The court can take cognizance of them only in a suit regularly brought before it, in which the point arises, and is essential to the rights of one of the parties." Precisely as the humblest Justice of the Peace would do. The debates in the Federal Convention show the exact meaning attached to the words of the Constitution, extending the judicial power of the United States to " all *cases* arising under the constitution, laws, and treaties of the United States." Mr. Madison feared that this might be interpreted to mean *questions,* but it was understood that the power given was "limited to *cases* of a judicial nature."—See Madison's debates, Elliot V., 483; also Curtis, who ably discusses this point, *Commentaries on the Jurisdiction of U. S. Courts,* I., 95.

of Jefferson, and has furnished at the same time a serious warning to all who prefer a government based upon law, to either despotism or anarchy.

The case of Dred Scott was the occasion taken by certain judges of the Supreme Court, to speak from the bench on matters not legally before them* — on matters which they had no right in their judicial capacity to discourse upon — which, *as judges*, they could not touch without encroaching upon the functions of the Legislature, nor as *individuals* without prostituting the dignity of their office; converting the Temple of Justice into another Tammany Hall, and the Supreme Bench into a caucus-platform. And one of these harangues, that of Mr. Taney, was but a short time after seized upon by the Chief Executive Magistrate of the country, treated by him as a decision, and made the justification of a particular line of policy; — a policy tending to make labor dishonorable in the Territories of the Republic.†

---

* " Many things were said by the court which are of no authority. Nothing which has been said by them, which has not a direct bearing on the jurisdiction of the court, against which they decided, can be considered as authority. *I shall certainly not regard it as such.* The question of jurisdiction being before the court was decided by them authoritatively, but nothing beyond that question."— Justice M'Lean, in *Dred Scott* v. *Sandford.* Howard's *Reports,* XIX. 549.

† I know of no eminent lawyer in the country who has sustained the declarations of the Chief Justice in this case. It has been asserted that the former Attorney-General of the United States, Mr. Caleb Cushing, whose profound learning and legal sagacity all admit, upholds them; but he is re-

To the honor of the judiciary, two judges, and they the most learned upon the bench, were found faithful among the faithless. Mr. Justice McLean, after

ported to have said, on the 27th February, 1858, in the Legislature of Massachusetts: " There are parts of the opinion of the court, which in his opinion could not be sustained," and then to have commented on those parts " from which he dissented." (See *Legislative debates* in *Boston Daily Advertiser*, 1st March, 1858.) On a subsequent day, Mr. Cushing being present, the following able analysis of the case was made by a member of less experience but of equal legal acumen, Mr. John A. Andrew, and the correctness of this analysis has never, that I am aware, been disproved by Mr. Cushing. Mr. Andrew said:

" On the question of the possibility of citizenship to one of Dred Scott's color, extraction and origin, three justices, viz. Taney, Wayne and Daniel, held the negative. Nelson and Campbell passed over the plea by which the question was raised. Grier agreed with Nelson. Catron said the question was not open. McLean agreed with Catron, but thought the plea bad. Curtis agreed that the question was open, but attacked the plea, met its averments, and decided that a free-born colored person, native to any State, is a citizen thereof, by birth, and is therefore a citizen of the Union, and entitled to sue in the Federal Courts. But three judges of the Supreme Court have, as yet, judicially denied the capacity of citizenship to such as Dred Scott and family.

" Had a majority of the court directly sustained the plea in abatement, and denied the jurisdiction of the Circuit Court appealed from, then all else they could have said and done would have been done and said in a cause not theirs to try and not theirs to discuss. In the absence of such majority, one step more was to be taken. And the next step reveals an agreement of six of the Justices, on a point decisive of the cause, and putting an end to all the functions of the court.

" It is this. Scott was first carred to Rock Island, in the State of Illinois, where he remained about two years, before going with his master to Fort Snelling, in the Territory of Wisconsin. His claim to freedom was rested on the alleged effect of his translation from a slave State, and again into a free Territory. If, by his removal to Illinois, he became emancipated from his master, the subsequent continuance of his pilgrimage into the Louisiana purchase could not add to his freedom, nor alter the fact. If, by reason of any want or infirmity in the laws of Illinois, or of conformity on his part to their behests, Dred Scott remained a slave while he remained in that State, then — for the sake of learning the effect on him of his territorial residence beyond the Mississippi, and of his marriage and other proceedings there ; and the effect of the sojournment and marriage of Harriet, in the same Territory, upon herself and her children — it might become needful to advance one other step into the investigation of the law ; to inspect the Missouri Compromise, banishing slavery to the south of the line of 36° 30' in the Louisiana purchase.

" But no exigency of the cause ever demanded or justified that advance ; for six of the Justices, including the Chief Justice himself, decided that the *status* of the plaintiff, as free or slave, was dependent, not upon the laws of the State into which he had been, but of the State of Missouri, in which he was at the commencement of the suit. The Chief Justice asserted that ' it is now firmly settled by the decisions of the highest court in the State, that Scott and his family, on their return were not free, but were, by the laws of Missouri, the property of the defendant.' This was the burden of the opinion of Nelson, who declares ' the question is one solely depending upon the law of Missouri, and that showing the dangerous novelty of the conduct of the court; its violation of precedent, of written law, and of natural right; and after declaring that the mere "sayings" of the court would not be regarded by him as authority, expressed his regret that its declaration of a year before (in Pease *v.* Peck, 18 Howard) did not seem to be fresh in the minds of some of his brethren: "that it could not yield its convictions

the federal Court sitting in the State, and trying the case before us, was bound to follow it.' It received the emphatic endorsement of Wayne, whose general concurrence was with the Chief Justice. Grier concurred in set terms with Nelson on all 'the questions discussed by him.' Campbell says, 'The claim of the plaintiff to freedom depends upon the effect to be given to his absence from Missouri, in company with his master in Illinois and Minnesota, *and this effect is to be ascertained by reference to the laws of Missouri.*' Five of the Justices then (if no more of them) regarded the law of Missouri as decisive of the plaintiff's rights.

"The Chief Justice and Justices Wayne and Nelson and Grier plainly hold that, on this point, the Court of the United States were bound to follow the decision of the Court of Missouri, which had already passed upon the question. And if Campbell did not intend to be bound by the Missouri Court, we are at a loss to understand what he does mean; since, asking 'what is the law of Missouri in such a case?' and, after citing Scott *v.* Emerson in the 15th of the Missouri Reports and various authorities of several States, he concludes that 'questions of *status* are closely connected with questions arising out of the social and political organization of the State where they originate, *and each sovereign power must determine them within its own territories.*' He held conclusively and distinctly, and so also did Mr. Justice Catron, in common with all the judges, besides McLean and Curtis, — on their own investigation and reasoning, — that the law of Missouri (to be ascertained either by themselves, or by exploring the declared opinion of the Courts,) must rule the cause. And they all affirm that, *irrespective of the law of Illinois and of the territory,* Scott was a slave by the law of Missouri, on his return within the confines of its jurisdiction.

"If the law of Illinois could have had no possible effect to secure freedom to Scott, when again remitted to Missouri, it follows that neither could the laws of the territory have availed him. The majority of the court had no occasion, therefore, to follow them into the territory, in order to look into the condition of Harriet and the children; because Dred, as a slave, could have no wife nor child, known to the law or recognized by the Court. But if any such occasion had existed, the same answer, — of the effect of the Missouri law, — was sufficient to control the cause.

"Here, then, we have a man, found by three of the Court, to be a person impossible to be a citizen, by reason of ancestral disabilities; by the same three, and four more of them, to have been *a slave,* by the law of his domicil at the inception of the suit. And yet, on the strength of observations and reflections indulged by a majority of these gentlemen, after their judicial functions had ceased for want of a competent plaintiff in the suit — for want of a man competent to the ownership of his own body, (on one side of their record,) — it is claimed by the President of the United States, that slavery 'exists in *Kansas under the Constitution of the United States,*' and that *this point has been declared by the highest tribunal known to our laws.*' "

8

where, after a long course of consistent decisions, some new light suddenly springs up, or an excited public opinion has elicited new doctrines subversive of former safe precedent." *

Mr. Justice Curtis declared that, without violating *duty*, he could not follow Mr. Taney in discussing matters not before the court; and, true to judicial principles, said, " he did not hold the opinion of that court, or any court binding, when expressed on a question not legitimately before it." He did not fail, however, thoroughly to examine the question *before* the court, and showed that upon that, the opinion of Mr. Chief Justice Taney was as illegal as was the demagogical harangue of Mr. Taney on matters *not before* the court.†

The Chief Justice had declared that, " every person, and every class and description of persons, who were at the time of the adoption of the Constitution recognized as citizens in the several States, became

---

* Howard XIX., 563.

† In the trial of Woodfall, the printer of Junius, the aberrations of the Chief Justice — less flagrant by far than those in the Dred Scott case — were, it will be remembered, the object of discussion in the House of Lords, where Lord Chatham, on the 11th of December, 1770, said : " The court are so confined to the record that they cannot take notice of anything that does not appear on the face of it ; in the legal phrase they cannot travel out of the record. The noble judge did travel out of the record ; and I affirm that his *discourse* was irregular, extra-judicial, and unprecedented. His apparent motive for doing what he knew to be wrong, was that he might have an opportunity of *telling the public* extra-judicially " certain things, which Chatham proceeds to develop.—Woodfall's *Junius*, I., 29.

also citizens of this new political body." * He asserted, however, that the free descendants of imported Africans " were at that time (viz., in 1787) considered as a subordinate and inferior class of beings," having no natural rights ;† that " they had for more than a century before been regarded as beings . . . so far inferior that they had no rights which the white man was bound to respect ; "‡ that " this was an axiom in morals as well as in politics ; " — from which premises he declared that they were not then citizens in the States (passing over in utter silence the statutes of several States prior to 1787, which made them citizens), and could not, therefore, be then, nor afterwards, citizens of the United States.§

Well did Mr. Justice Curtis overthrow this monstrous assertion, by pointing to the laws of five States, among them North Carolina, which, in 1787, gave to

---

* Howard XIX., 406.

† " No rights or privileges but such as those who held the power and the government might grant them."—C. J. Taney, in Howard XIX., 405.

‡ Howard XIX., 407.

§ This paragraph is the careful condensation of twenty-four pages of casuistry in the official report of the opinion of the court.—*Ibid*, 403–427. The marginal summary of the official reporter stands thus: " When the Constitution was adopted, they [*i. e.*, freemen of the African race, whose ancestors were brought to this country and sold] were not regarded in any of the States as members of the community which constituted the State, and were not numbered among its ' people or citizens ' ; consequently the special rights and immunities guaranteed to citizens do not apply to them. And, not being ' citizens ' within the meaning of the Constitution, they are not entitled to sue in that character in a court of the United States."—*Ibid*, 393.

free colored men the full rights of citizens, enforcing
this by the decision of Judge Gaston, of North Carolina. He also cited the Articles of Confederation of
1778, the fourth of which declared the "free inhabitants of each of these States entitled to all the
privileges and immunities of free citizens in the
several States;" he showed by the discussions in Congress at the time, that the question was then thoroughly
understood; and pointed out the efforts of South
Carolina to so amend this article as to restrict citizenship to whites, efforts in which only one of the
thirteen States joined her.* Mr. Justice Curtis might
also have cited the statute of Virginia of 1783, which
declares that all freemen are citizens, and which repeals the law of 1779, that limited citizenship to
whites.

Carrying the opinion of the Chief Justice to its
logical result, Mr. Justice Curtis showed that it implied the power to change our Republic to "an oli-
garchy, in whose hands would be concentrated the
entire power of the Federal Government."

Against doctrines and conduct so destructive to
our free institutions, it behoves us all, on this day,
solemnly to protest. On this day again, it behoves
us to remember, that an injury done to the humblest
among us, whatever his color, whatever the country
of his birth, is an injury done to us all.

* Howard XIX., 572–5.

All who believe in natural rights, and all who
uphold existing things, are here called upon to act.
In presence of usurpation, it becomes most especially
the duty of all conservative men of the country to
come forward.

I honor the conservative who stands the guardian
of order, of existing rights, and of instituted liberty,
and who gracefully yields at last to the progress of
an advancing civilization :

" Who serves the right, and yields to *right* alone."

But there are some who, calling themselves conservatives, conserve nothing, and who yield, not to the
advances of civilization, but to the encroachments of
barbarism ; whose whole conservatism is constant con-
cession ; who tell us they are " as much opposed to
barbarism as any one," but they wouldn't meet it on
the field of politics, — " as much opposed to crime
as any one," but they wouldn't hear a warning voice
raised against it from the pulpit; — their politics are
too pure, their Sunday slumbers too precious, to be
disturbed by any allusions to such exciting matters
as the advances of crime. And so they go on, con-
ceding everything, — not to civilization, but to barbarism, — not to liberty, but to liberticide — backing
down before every presumptuous aggression—down—
and down still — until they fall among the lost ones

whom Dante has described.* From them there is nothing to expect.

"Non ragionam di lor, ma guarda e passa."

We have, however, among us some real conservatives, and many intelligent and worthy men, who neglect the privileges, shall I not say the duties, of citizenship, and who, either from indifference or from a false fastidiousness, abstain from the polls. To these men I would, on this occasion, specially appeal. You complain that your vote is only that of one, and that however great your intelligence, however profound your learning, it may all be outweighed by the vote of the most simple. Here then is an opportunity for effective action; here is the occasion foreseen by the sagacious Story, when he placed the security against a trespass by the Supreme Court upon the known principles of law, in the intelligence, the integrity, the learning and the manliness of the country, which would keep watch upon its proceedings.

Here you may exercise your knowledge, and the

* " —— Master,
What wretched souls are these in anguish drowned?"
To which he answered, " This award severe
On those unhappy spirits is bestowed,
Of whom nor infamy nor good was known,
Joined with that wicked crew which unto God
Nor false nor faithful, served themselves alone."
Inferno: Canto III., Parsons's Trans.

influence which it may carry with it. Bring that knowledge and influence to bear upon the judges who have acquiesced in that deplorable prostitution of their office ; aid them to see the error of their ways; point out to them the fountains of that law of which they are the ministers ; draw them gently back to an appreciation of those elementary principles of jurisprudence, and of judicial action, which seem to have passed from their memories; furnish the Chief Justice with a copy of the decisions of North Carolina and of the statutes of Virginia ;* persuade him to read the history of his country ; tell them all, not in anger but in sorrow, of the disastrous consequences of their example ; show to them that whatever factitious popularity may follow their conduct, the wise and the good are not with them, and that— though they may have a Senate at their heels ready to print and circulate their opinions through the country at the public expense — the voices of all the true and enlightened will condemn them in the present,

---

* Particularly the 11th volume of " Hening's Virginia Statutes," where on p. 322 may be found the law of October, 1783, which repeals that of 1779, limiting citizenship to whites, and which enacts, " That all *free* persons, born within the territory of this Commonwealth shall be deemed *citizens* of this Commonwealth." To this might be joined the opinion of the learned Judge Gaston, of North Carolina, (4 Dev. and Bat. 20), cited by Justice Curtis (19 Howard, 573) : " All free persons born within the State are born citizens of the State. It is a matter of universal notoriety, that under the Constitution of North Carolina, free persons, without regard to color, claimed and exercised the franchise."

and the Muse of History chronicle their names in the black catalogue of unworthy judges.

And if with all this you find them deaf to your remonstrances, unwilling to purify the ermine which, confided to them, has been draggled and soiled, if, unconscious of

> " —— their foul disfigurement,
> They boast themselves more comely than before,"

you will at least have the satisfaction of knowing that you have done something to serve your country.

But this conduct of the court, though at first it may most shock the student of history, and the jurist, conversant with those principles which through the long struggle between arbitrary power and right have been evolved as the guaranties of justice between man and man, this usurpation on the part of the judiciary comes home to every one; to the rich as well as to the poor; to the powerful as well as to the weak; to the wise as well as to the simple; to the white as well as to the black.

To-day liberty is attacked; to-morrow it may be property. Let this be calmly acquiesced in, and no interest however respectable, no right however sacred, is safe. In opposition to the monstrous conduct of these judges all of us may cordially unite: in this all shades of party may blend; for no party, however strong it may appear, however great the selfish interests it may suppose to be flattered, no party can long bear up under the opprobrium of a measure which tends to undermine our institutions; which destroys the harmonious balance of the power delegated by the people to different branches of their government, and leads logically on to despotism or to revolution.

Let us, therefore, all join our efforts to restore the purity of the judiciary, — to aid it to recover its self-respect; and having done this, let us prove that our celebration of this day is no mere empty show, by honoring the immortal truths of the Declaration, and by earnestly endeavoring in the future to act up to them. Let us rally around the Constitution of our country, which guarantees trial by jury to all, and which, in its own words, was "ordained to establish justice, and secure the blessings of liberty;" let us drive far away the corruption in power, and make JUSTICE and LIBERTY the persistent rule of action of our government.

Then shall we offer an acceptable tribute to the memory of those who founded our Republic; then shall our country present a cheering example to other nations struggling with oppression; then, true to itself, it shall be stationed,

> "Like a beneficent star for all to gaze at,
>   So high and glowing, that kingdoms far and foreign,
>   Shall by it read their destiny."

THE DINNER AT FANEUIL HALL.

AFTER the Oration, the City Authorities and their guests dined in Faneuil Hall. From the official account of the ceremonies of the day, are extracted the following remarks made at the dinner by a guest of the City, Mr. Palfrey, of New Orleans, and by Mr. Sumner.

Mr. PALFREY, having been called upon by the Mayor to reply to the sixth regular sentiment, among other things, said :

" It is peculiarly a hard case for a man who has been a citizen of the South for fifty years, who is an American citizen, and enjoys the protection of the Stars and Stripes, to return to his native city and hear such sentiments promulgated as I have been obliged to listen to in the Music Hall to-day."

The seventh regular sentiment, given by the Mayor, immediately after this, was —

The Orator of the Day — His eloquent address adds fresh laurels to the name of Sumner, already twice distinguished by his father and brother on the roll of the orators of Boston.

Mr. GEORGE SUMNER, being called upon by the Mayor, responded as follows :

"I am deeply grateful, Mr. Mayor and Fellow-Citizens, for the manner in which this sentiment has been received, as it shows that the memory of my honored father, and the name of my absent brother, are fresh in your minds. The allusion to my father gratifies not alone my filial feelings, but those which I have as a citizen of Boston, glad to see honor rendered to every example of integrity, justice and patriotism. You have spoken of him as one of the orators of Boston. May I be permitted to recall an occasion (not the fourth of July) on which, as it seems to me, he spoke also for Boston, and with a certain eloquence.

"In 1812, the dominant interest of our city was strongly opposed to a war with England. At that time, a call was made for a national loan, and subscription books were sent to Boston. These were received in no complimentary manner. In that street which witnessed the first conflict between British troops and American citizens, it was stated that no money would be given in Boston — and, moreover, that any one who subscribed to the loan should be stigmatized. These menaces had their effect. Days rolled on, no money came, and the jeers of the street were redoubled. At that moment, my father, then a young lawyer, sold some property, got together what money he could command, paid it to the agent of the national treasury, and put his name, solitary and alone, upon the stigmatized list.

"Two days after, the impulsive, warm-hearted, civic hero of our Revolution, in whom the spirit of party never rose superior to patriotism, the venerable John Adams, came from Quincy and put his name also on the list.

"The subscription of my father was not large — it was the young lawyer's mite — but in standing forward when the national honor had been attacked, and in doing a patriotic act, in presence of menace, there was a civic courage, which I may, perhaps, be pardoned for remember-

ing with a certain satisfaction. On that occasion, it seems
to me that he was the real orator of Boston, speaking by
action, not perhaps the dominant or the fashionable sentiment of the moment, but the sober second-thought of
this great city; which is always true to the national honor,
and true to the principles of the founders of the Republic.

" I shall not follow the gentleman who has just preceded
me in any discussion. This is Faneuil Hall, and this is
the City of Boston. I congratulate him on being where
every man is free to express his opinions. In so much
of what I have had the honor to say this day in another
place, as regards recent events in our own country, I am
supported by Jefferson, by Hamilton, by Story, and by
the great jurist of Louisiana, Edward Livingston. With
them I am content to stand or fall.

" In every part of Europe, but more especially in France,
I have remarked, Mr. Mayor, the honor paid to our native
city. Landing at Boulogne, I found myself passing through
the *rue de Boston;* and in two other cities of France found
the dear old name upon street corners. This honor is thus
rendered on account of the example given by Boston in
her sacrifices for liberty; and because she has always
recognized the necessity of basing her liberty firmly upon
law; and as the guaranty of this, *of keeping the legislative,
executive and judicial functions separated from each other.*

" Permit me, sir, to propose as a sentiment:

" *The City of Boston* — The first to make sacrifices for the liberties
of the whole country; the firmest in maintaining the UNION formed
to secure the blessings of LIBERTY to all."